GAULISH VILLAGE

COMPENDIUM

LAUDANUM

AQUARIUM

TOTORUM

BELGICA

• LUTETIA

ARMORICA

GAUL
(ROMAN CONQUEST)
50 BC
CELTICA

AQUITANIA

PROVINCIA

THE YEAR IS 50 BC. GAUL IS ENTIRELY OCCUPIED BY THE
ROMANS. WELL, NOT ENTIRELY ... ONE SMALL VILLAGE OF
INDOMITABLE GAULS STILL HOLDS OUT AGAINST THE INVADERS.
AND LIFE IS NOT EASY FOR THE ROMAN LEGIONARIES WHO
GARRISON THE FORTIFIED CAMPS OF TOTORUM, AQUARIUM,
LAUDANUM AND COMPENDIUM ...

ASTERIX, THE HERO OF THESE ADVENTURES. A SHREWD, CUNNING LITTLE WARRIOR, ALL PERILOUS MISSIONS ARE IMMEDIATELY ENTRUSTED TO HIM. ASTERIX GETS HIS SUPERHUMAN STRENGTH FROM THE MAGIC POTION BREWED BY THE DRUID GETAFIX . . .

OBELIX, ASTERIX'S INSEPARABLE FRIEND. A MENHIR DELIVERY MAN BY TRADE, ADDICTED TO WILD BOAR. OBELIX IS ALWAYS READY TO DROP EVERYTHING AND GO OFF ON A NEW ADVENTURE WITH ASTERIX – SO LONG AS THERE'S WILD BOAR TO EAT, AND PLENTY OF FIGHTING. HIS CONSTANT COMPANION IS DOGMATIX, THE ONLY KNOWN CANINE ECOLOGIST, WHO HOWLS WITH DESPAIR WHEN A TREE IS CUT DOWN.

GETAFIX, THE VENERABLE VILLAGE DRUID, GATHERS MISTLETOE AND BREWS MAGIC POTIONS. HIS SPECIALITY IS THE POTION WHICH GIVES THE DRINKER SUPERHUMAN STRENGTH. BUT GETAFIX ALSO HAS OTHER RECIPES UP HIS SLEEVE . . .

CACOFONIX, THE BARD. OPINION IS DIVIDED AS TO HIS MUSICAL GIFTS. CACOFONIX THINKS HE'S A GENIUS. EVERY-ONE ELSE THINKS HE'S UNSPEAKABLE. BUT SO LONG AS HE DOESN'T SPEAK, LET ALONE SING, EVERYBODY LIKES HIM . . .

FINALLY, VITALSTATISTIX, THE CHIEF OF THE TRIBE. MAJESTIC, BRAVE AND HOT-TEMPERED, THE OLD WARRIOR IS RESPECTED BY HIS MEN AND FEARED BY HIS ENEMIES. VITALSTATISTIX HIMSELF HAS ONLY ONE FEAR, HE IS AFRAID THE SKY MAY FALL ON HIS HEAD TOMORROW. BUT AS HE ALWAYS SAYS, TOMORROW NEVER COMES.

IN THE YEAR 50 BC, AFTER A LONG STRUGGLE, THE ANCIENT GAULS HAD BEEN CONQUERED BY THE ROMANS...

CHIEFS LIKE VERCINGETORIX HAD TO LAY THEIR ARMS AT CAESAR'S FEET...

OUCH!

CLANG!

PEACE REIGNS, DISTURBED ONLY BY OCCASIONAL ATTACKS BY THE GERMANS, SPEEDILY REPULSED...

So! But ve komm back!

Gut! Ve go!

ALL GAUL IS OCCUPIED...

BELGICA

ARMORICA

CELTICA

AQUITANIA

PROVINCIA

ALL? NO — ONE VILLAGE STILL HOLDS OUT STUBBORNLY AGAINST THE INVADERS. ONE SMALL VILLAGE SURROUNDED BY FORTIFIED ROMAN CAMPS...

1A

COMPENDIUM

AQUARIUM

LAUDANUM

TOTORUM

ALL EFFORTS TO SUBDUE THESE PROUD GAULS HAVE FAILED AND CAESAR ASKS HIMSELF ...

QUID?

AND NOW WE MEET OUR HERO, THE WARRIOR ASTERIX, JUST OFF HUNTING AS USUAL ...

BACK SOON, ASTERIX?

I'LL BE BACK FOR DINNER, OBELIX.

HERE HE COMES!

WE'LL GET HIM.

IPSO FACTO!

SIC!

BIFF!

OW!

BANG!

OUCH!

ACCIDENCE WILL HAPPEN...

VAE VICTO VAE VICTIS!

WE DECLINE!

1B

5

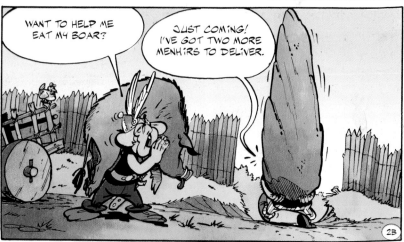

6

COME IN, OBELIX. IT'S DONE TO A TURN!

YUM, YUM, ASTERIX!

THE ROMANS WON'T LIKE THIS. THEY'LL LAUNCH A NEW OFFENSIVE...

HUH!

SO LONG AS OUR DRUID GETAFIX KEEPS BREWING HIS MAGIC POTION, THE ROMANS CAN'T DO A THING.

LET'S GO AND SEE THE DRUID NOW!

HE'LL BE UP THAT TREE, CUTTING MISTLETOE WITH HIS GOLDEN SICKLE.

TCHIC! TCHAC!

3A

GETAFIX! O DRUID!

OWW!

YOU MADE ME JUMP! I'VE GONE AND CUT MYSELF WITH MY SICKLE.

SORRY...

THE TIME HAS COME FOR ME TO HAVE MY DOSE OF POTION...

OH, ALL RIGHT...

COME HOME WITH ME.....

3B

7

HERE IS THE POTION THAT MAKES THE DRINKER INVINCIBLE! IT INCREASES HIS STRENGTH TENFOLD – FOR A LIMITED PERIOD OF TIME.

WHAT'S THE RECIPE, O DRUID?

THE ORIGIN OF THIS RECIPE IS LOST IN THE MISTS OF TIME. IT IS HANDED DOWN FROM DRUID TO DRUID BY WORD OF MOUTH...

ALL I CAN REVEAL IS THAT THERE'S MISTLETOE AND LOBSTER IN IT...

THE LOBSTER IS OPTIONAL, BUT IT IMPROVES THE FLAVOUR!

SPLOSH!

4A

CAN I HAVE SOME?

NO, OBELIX, YOU CAN NOT AND WELL YOU KNOW IT!

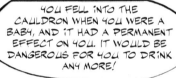

YOU FELL INTO THE CAULDRON WHEN YOU WERE A BABY, AND IT HAD A PERMANENT EFFECT ON YOU. IT WOULD BE DANGEROUS FOR YOU TO DRINK ANY MORE!

GLUG! GLUG! GLUG!

THANKS, O DRUID!

IT'S NOT FAIR, BY BELENOS!

OW! OW! OW!

I'VE TOLD YOU BEFORE NOT TO SHAKE HANDS WITH ME WHEN YOU'VE JUST HAD YOUR POTION.

HE'S RIGHT, I DON'T KNOW MY OWN STRENGTH!

4B

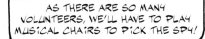

9

(†) SPAGHETTI WAS NOT IMPORTED FROM CHINA BY MARCO POLO UNTIL MUCH LATER.

MARCUS GINANTONICUS AND HIS HEROIC DETACHMENT RETURN TO COMPENDIUM...

TCHIC! BLDZRRRLM MTDZRNIIM NZDRC

THE GAULS CAME AND SAW AND CONQUERED CALIGULA MINUS!

10A

A GREAT VICTORY FOR US!

LET'S HOPE CALIGULA MINUS GETS BACK IN ONE PIECE TO TELL US WHAT HE'S SEEN!

HE'D BETTER! IF NOT I'LL HAVE SOMETHING TO SAY TO HIS ROMAN REMAINS!

ALEA JACTA EST!

PARDON?

MEANWHILE...

THIS IS OUR VILLAGE, CALIGULIMINIX. YOU'LL BE SAFE HERE! IT'S FULL OF GAULS!

THAT'S A GREAT COMFORT.

ASTERIX AND OBELIX ARE BACK!

THEY'VE GOT SOMETHING WITH THEM!

SOMETHING VERY PECULIAR, BY BELENOS!

COME AND MEET OUR CHIEF, VITALSTATISTIX.

BUT – BUT THEY'RE ALL ARMED!

YES, WE HAVE TO BE PREPARED TO FIGHT THE ROMANS AT THE DROP OF A HELMET.

A WISE PRECAUTION!

10B

14

DINNER'S READY, CALIGULIMINIX. IT'S WILD BOAR!

IS THERE SOME SECRET BEHIND YOUR SUPERHUMAN STRENGTH?

YUM! YUM! YES BUT WE CAN'T REVEAL IT! SCRUNCH!

EAT UP YOUR BOAR, IT'S GETTING COLD.

WHY CAN'T YOU REVEAL YOUR SECRET?

BECAUSE IT'S A SECRET!

THAT'S NOT FAIR! WHAT ARE THINGS COMING TO IF ONE GAUL CAN'T TRUST ANOTHER?

?

IF I WAS AS STRONG AS YOU I COULD GET THROUGH THE ROMAN LINES AND GO HOME TO LUTETIA!

!

12A

MY POOR FAMILY! SNIFF! THEY'LL BE WORRIED TO DEATH!

WHAT DO WE DO NOW?

WE COULD ALWAYS EAT HIS WILD BOAR?

COME ON, CALIGULIMINIX! WE'RE GOING TO SEE THE DRUID.

HE'LL BE UP AN OAK TREE. IT'S THE SIXTH DAY OF THE NEW MOON, AND MISTLETOE CUT THEN IS A POWERFUL ANTIDOTE TO POISON.

HI, DRUID!

OUCH!

ASTERIX, I TOLD YOU BEFORE NOT TO MAKE ME JUMP WHEN I'M USING MY SICKLE!!!

12B

16

COME ON, ALL OF YOU! OUR DRUID GETAFIX IS GOING TO MAKE THE MAGIC POTION!

ONE PORTION OF THIS POTION WILL GIVE YOU ALL THE STRENGTH YOU NEED TO GET HOME TO LUTETIA...

...BUT THE EFFECTS WILL WEAR OFF QUITE QUICKLY

NEVER MIND, I'LL SEE ABOUT STEALING THAT CAULDRON!

HERE'S THE POTION!

THIS POTION... I... ER, I POTATE IT?

GLUG! GLUG! GLUG! GLUG! GLUG!

TASTES LIKE VEGETABLE SOUP!

IT COMES IN SEVERAL OTHER DELICIOUS FLAVOURS: SHRIMP, CHEESE OMELETTE, DUCK WITH ORANGE SAUCE AND VANILLA!

BUT I DON'T FEEL ANY DIFFERENT...

TRY LIFTING THAT ROCK OVER THERE!

THIS ONE? BUT I COULD NEVER...

?!!?

HA! HA! HA!

HA! HA!

HA! HA!

HA! HA! HA! HA!

18

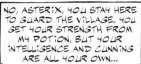

26

HERE WE ARE IN THE CAMP! ARE YOU GOING TO PLAY YOUR PRACTICAL JOKE NOW?

NO, IT'S GETTING DARK. I'LL WAIT TILL MORNING, IT'LL BE FUNNIER THEN.

OH!

GOOD NIGHT!

SOON AFTERWARDS

AND NOW TO FIND WHERE THEY'VE GOT THE DRUID...

ZZZZz

LET'S HAVE A LOOK OVER HERE...

23A

RECLINE AND HAVE A BITE TO EAT, O MARCUS GINANTONICUS, MY TRUSTY NUMBER TWO. I WANT A WORD WITH YOU!

THANKS, O CRISMUS BONUS!

WE MUST GET THE DRUID'S RECIPE! WITH IT WE SHALL BE INVINCIBLE. WE CAN GO TO ROME AND TAKE OVER FROM CAESAR!

JULIUS

CAESAR?

PRECISELY, JULIUS! THE TWO OF US WILL FORM A TRIUMVIRATE!

I NEED YOU NOW, BUT AFTERWARDS I'LL BE THE TRIUMVIRATE ON MY OWN!

I'LL HAVE HIM THROWN TO THE LIONS, AND THEN I ALONE WILL BE CAESAR!

23B

30

IT'S DAYS SINCE THE MESSENGERS LEFT TO LOOK FOR STRAWBERRIES, AND NOT ONE HAS TURNED UP YET!

THE MESSENGERS ARE BACK, O CRISMUS BONUS!

ABOUT TIME!

AVE CRISMUS BONUS!

AVE, AVE, BOYS! THE STRAWBERRIES – DID YOU GET THEM?

NO

NOT A STRAWBERRY.

WE LOOKED EVERYWHERE!

TULLIUS OCTOPUS ISN'T BACK YET.

29A

HERE I AM, O CRISMUS BONUS!

I FOUND STRAWBERRIES, O CRISMUS BONUS! I BOUGHT THEM FOR A VAST SUM FROM A GREEK MERCHANT I HAPPENED TO MEET!

GIVE THEM HERE!

THIS TIME I REALLY MEAN IT! AS A REWARD YOU CAN GO HOME ON LEAVE TO SEE ALL THE FUN OF THE CIRCUS!

I'M GOING TO THE CIRCUS! I'M GOING TO THE CIRCUS!

DRUID! HERE ARE THE STRAWBERRIES YOU ORDERED FOR THE MAGIC POTION!

WHAT DO YOU THINK OF THEM, ASTERIX?

NOT UP TO MUCH!

!

NOT BAD...

H.M...

29B

COME TO THINK OF IT, THOSE WERE EXCELLENT STRAWBERRIES!

YES, JUST THE SORT I NEED. GO AND GET ME SOME MORE.

WELL, IF YOU DON'T NEED ME ANY MORE I'LL BE OFF...

GEE UP!

33A

WAIT A MINUTE! IF I GOT IT RIGHT, I'M VERY STRONG NOW!

THIS IS GREAT! NOW I CAN SELL MY OXEN AND PULL THE CART MYSELF!

THAT POTION...

...CERTAINLY DOES HAVE...

...MAGIC POWERS!

AND AT COMPENDIUM...

GLUG GLUG GLUG GLUG!

COME ON, EVERYONE! LET'S ALL DRINK THE MAGIC POTION!

33B

37

40

41

I GIVE IN! GIVE ME THE ANTIDOTE AND YOU CAN GO FREE!

TRY A HAIR OF THE DOG?

GETAFIX MAY NOT REMEMBER THE ANTIDOTE...

HE'S A BIT HARE-BRAINED SOMETIMES!

HO! HO! HO!

POE! POE!

DON'T DISTRESS YOURSELF! WE AGREE!

I'LL HAVE TO GO AND FETCH INGREDIENTS FROM THE FOREST...

I'LL ARRANGE FOR AN ESCORT...

!

I MAY NOT HAVE THE SECRET OF THE MAGIC POTION, BUT AS SOON AS I'VE GOT RID OF THIS HAIR I'LL WIPE OUT THOSE TWO GAULS. IT WILL GIVE ME MORAL SATISFACTION!

38A

WHY WERE YOU SO QUICK TO ACCEPT HIS OFFER? THAT CENTURION MEANS MISCHIEF!

THE EFFECTS OF THE HAIR LOTION DON'T LAST LONG...

TOMORROW THEIR HAIR WILL HAVE STOPPED GROWING. I MUST THINK OF A WAY OUT OF THIS!

REPORTING TO ESCORT YOU TO THE FOREST FOR INGREDIENTS!

STOP WALKING ON MY HAIR!

WELL, PICK IT UP, THEN!

I HAVE A PLAN!

THAT'S OUR STRONG POINT, WE'RE BURSTING WITH IDEAS!

38B

42

43

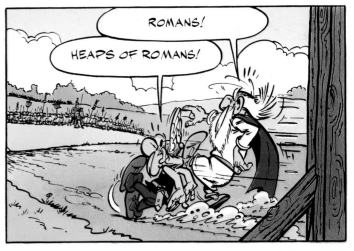

46

THE END

48